AF228607

DISCOVER BIOLOGY

Genetics

BY EMMA HUDDLESTON

CONTENT CONSULTANT
MERCEDES BURNS, PhD
ASSISTANT PROFESSOR
DEPARTMENT OF BIOLOGICAL SCIENCES
UNIVERSITY OF MARYLAND, BALTIMORE COUNTY

Kids Core
An Imprint of Abdo Publishing
abdobooks.com

abdobooks.com

Published by Abdo Publishing, a division of ABDO, PO Box 398166, Minneapolis, Minnesota 55439. Copyright © 2022 by Abdo Consulting Group, Inc. International copyrights reserved in all countries. No part of this book may be reproduced in any form without written permission from the publisher. Kids Core™ is a trademark and logo of Abdo Publishing.

Printed in the United States of America, North Mankato, Minnesota
052021
092021

Cover Photo: Shutterstock Images
Interior Photos: DTeibe Photography/Shutterstock Images, 4–5; Shutterstock Images, 6, 10, 12–13, 18–19, 23, 29; Monkey Business Images/iStockphoto, 9; Biophoto Associates/Science Source, 15; Lyubov Levitskaya/Shutterstock Images, 16; Fancy Tapis/Shutterstock Images, 20; Olga Ovcharenko/Shutterstock Images, 22; Nattakorn Maneerat/Shutterstock Images, 25; Monkey Business Images/Shutterstock Images, 26

Editor: Marie Pearson
Series Designer: Katharine Hale

Library of Congress Control Number: 2020948453

Publisher's Cataloging-in-Publication Data

Names: Huddleston, Emma, author.
Title: Genetics / by Emma Huddleston
Description: Minneapolis, Minnesota : Abdo Publishing, 2022 | Series: Discover biology | Includes online resources and index.
Identifiers: ISBN 9781532195334 (lib. bdg.) | ISBN 9781098215644 (ebook)
Subjects: LCSH: Biology--Juvenile literature. | Genetics--Juvenile literature. | Life sciences--Juvenile literature. | Evolution (Biology)--Juvenile literature.
Classification: DDC 575.1--dc23

CONTENTS

CHAPTER 1
One in the Litter 4

CHAPTER 2
Genes and Traits 12

CHAPTER 3
Inheriting Traits 18

Picture Biology 28
Glossary 30
Online Resources 31
Learn More 31
Index 32
About the Author 32

Puppies in the same litter can
be different colors.

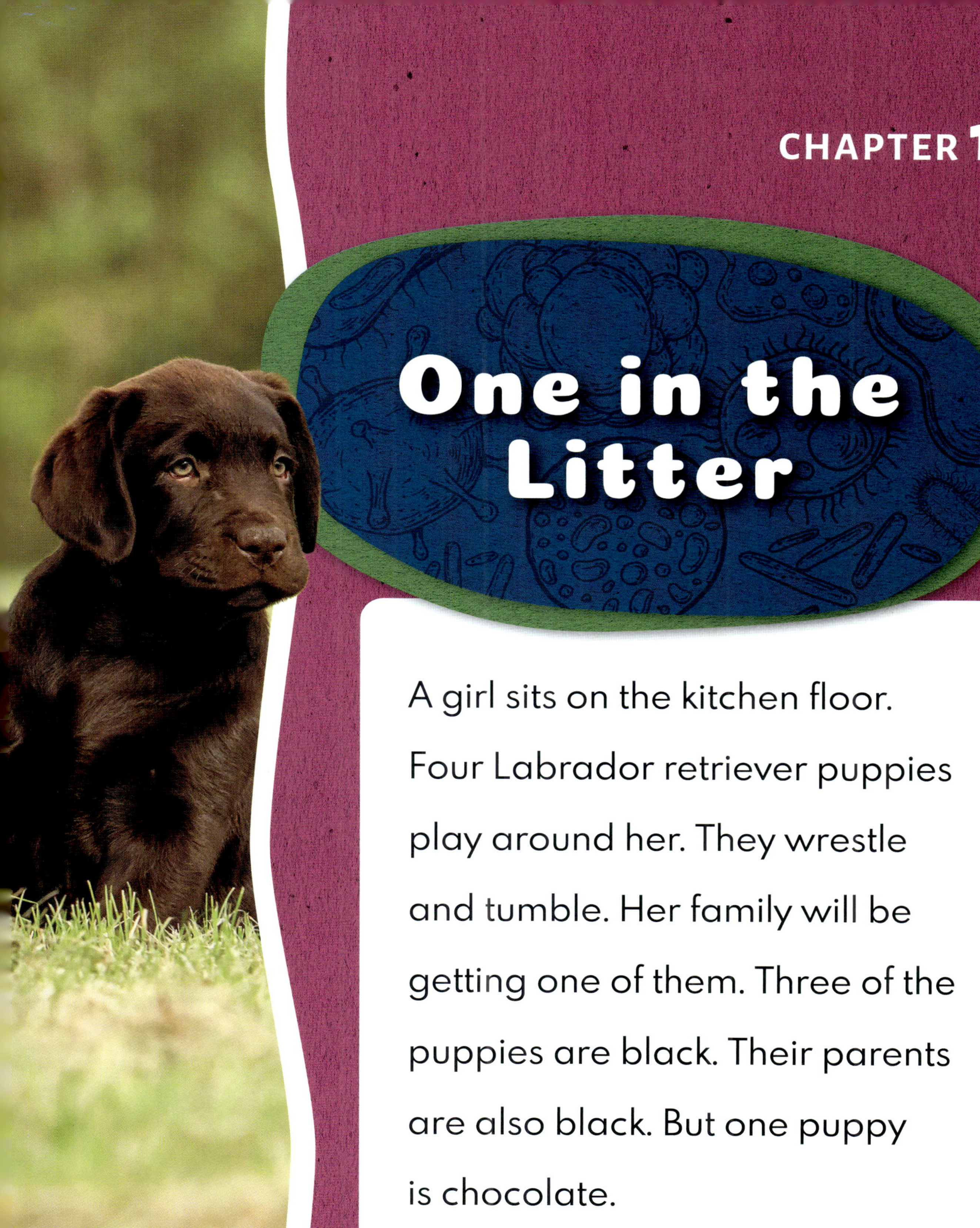

One in the Litter

A girl sits on the kitchen floor. Four Labrador retriever puppies play around her. They wrestle and tumble. Her family will be getting one of them. Three of the puppies are black. Their parents are also black. But one puppy is chocolate.

Genetics explains why puppies sometimes have different colors than their parents.

The girl wonders why the chocolate puppy looks different. Where did the color come from?

The breeder explains that it all has to do with **genes**. The chocolate-colored puppy still got its color from its parents. A dog's genes control whether its fur is black or chocolate. Both parents have one black gene and one chocolate gene. They each pass one gene to their puppies. That means there are three possibilities. A puppy could have two black genes. It could have two chocolate genes. Or it could have one of each. Just one black gene makes the fur black.

The chocolate puppy got a chocolate gene from both parents. It doesn't have any black genes. So it is brown.

What Is Genetics?

Genetics is the study of genes and how they are passed from parents to offspring. Genes act like instructions. They tell a body how to look. Sometimes they tell a body how to behave. They are part of every cell. Cells are tiny building blocks that make up all living things.

Scientists work to understand what makes humans different from each other and other

The Scoop on Cells

Trillions of cells make up the human body. Cells can grow. They can make copies of themselves. Cells have many parts. The **nucleus** is the command center of the cell. That is because it holds the genes. It gives directions to the other parts of the cell.

Genes are what make people similar in some ways and unique in others.

living things. So they study the human **genome**. A genome is all of an individual's genes together. Scientists want to know the role of each gene.

Children get a combination of their parents' genes.

Almost every living thing gets half its genes from its father. The other half comes from its mother. Every human has about 30,000 to 40,000 genes. Genes can explain why living things act and look the way they do.

Sir John Sulston was a genetic scientist. He researched the human genome. Sulston explained the goal of his research:

> [The human genome] is a very basic set of instructions and we have got to learn how our growing bodies interpret these instructions to make a human being.

Source: Tim Radford. "Door Opens on Deeper Mysteries." *Guardian*, 12 Feb. 2001, theguardian.com. Accessed 29 Apr. 2020.

Comparing Texts

Think about the quote. Does it support the information in this chapter? Or does it give a different perspective? Explain how in two to three sentences.

A gene is one section of a DNA strand. A strand of DNA forms a helix shape. It looks like a twisted ladder.

CHAPTER 2

Genes and Traits

A gene is a piece of DNA. DNA is a chemical. It is made of special acids. Each type of gene has a unique combination of acids. Genes are located on chromosomes. Chromosomes are tightly packed clumps of DNA.

Chromosomes are in a cell's **nucleus**. The nucleus controls cell activity similar to how the brain controls the body. Humans typically have 23 pairs of chromosomes in each cell. Most chromosomes have four arms. The arms form an X shape.

For human females, the twenty-third pair is made of two Xs. Males have one X and one Y shape. People get an X chromosome from

DNA Explained

DNA is made of four acidic bases. They are guanine, cytosine, adenine, and thymine. The pattern of the bases makes a code. The code gives the cells information, such as how to make the body grow.

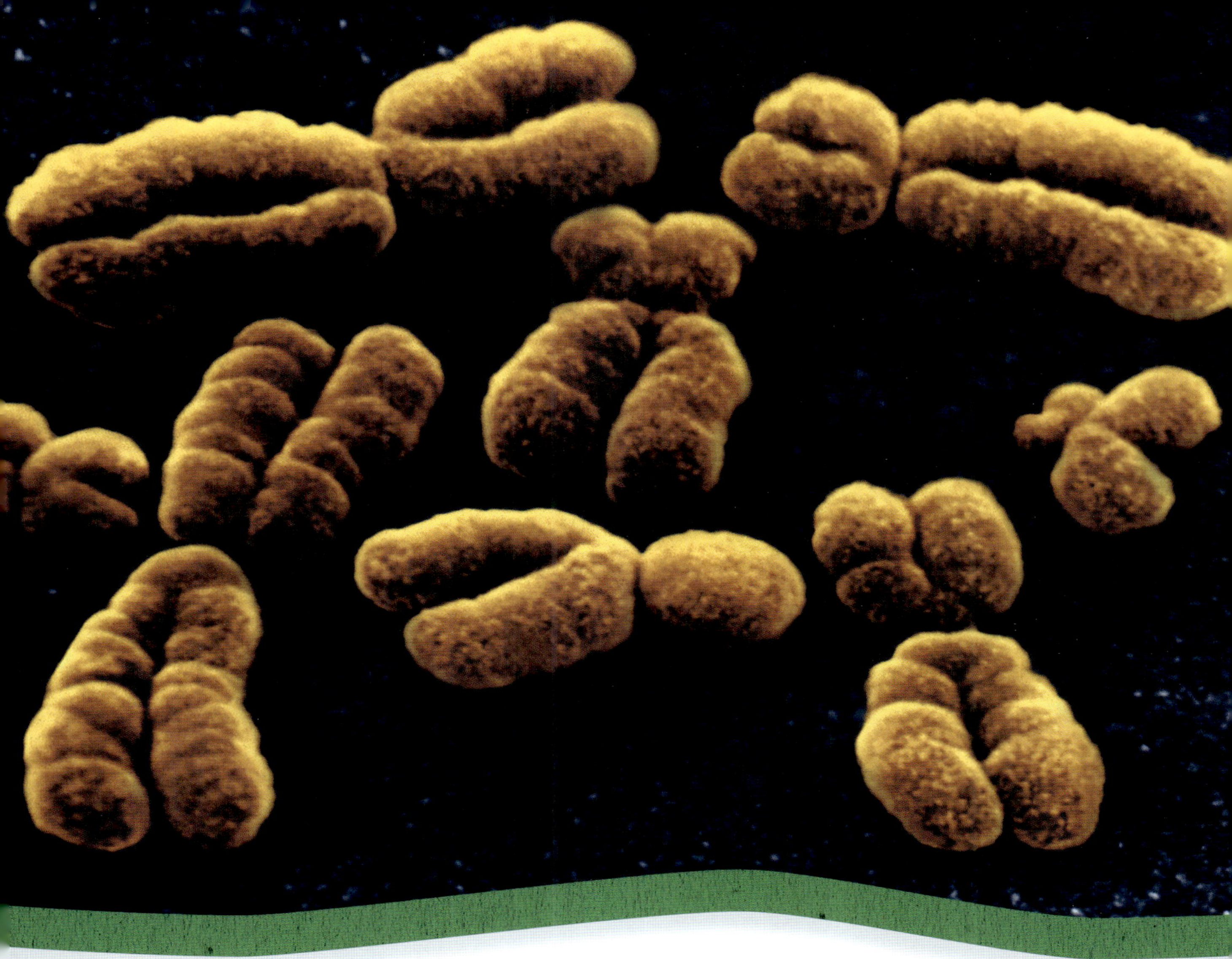

Chromosomes are very tiny. They can only be seen with a microscope.

their mother. If they get an X from their father, they will be female. If they get a Y, they will be male.

There is more to genetics than just DNA code, which is why identical twins are not exactly alike.

Traits

Genes influence traits. Traits can be anything from looks to behavior. Eye color and height are traits. The way people fold their hands can also be a trait.

Some traits, such as hair color, are fully **inherited**. They depend only on genes. Genes only partially influence other traits, such as shyness. These traits may change depending on how a person is raised. The combination of traits is unique for each person.

Further Evidence

Look at the website below. Does it give any new evidence about genes to support Chapter Two?

Heredity: Who Are You?

abdocorelibrary.com/genetics

Parents' genes make it more
likely that their offspring will
have certain traits over others.

CHAPTER 3

Inheriting Traits

People can predict the likelihood of offspring getting a certain trait from parents. A Punnett square helps with finding those odds. This square has four or more sections.

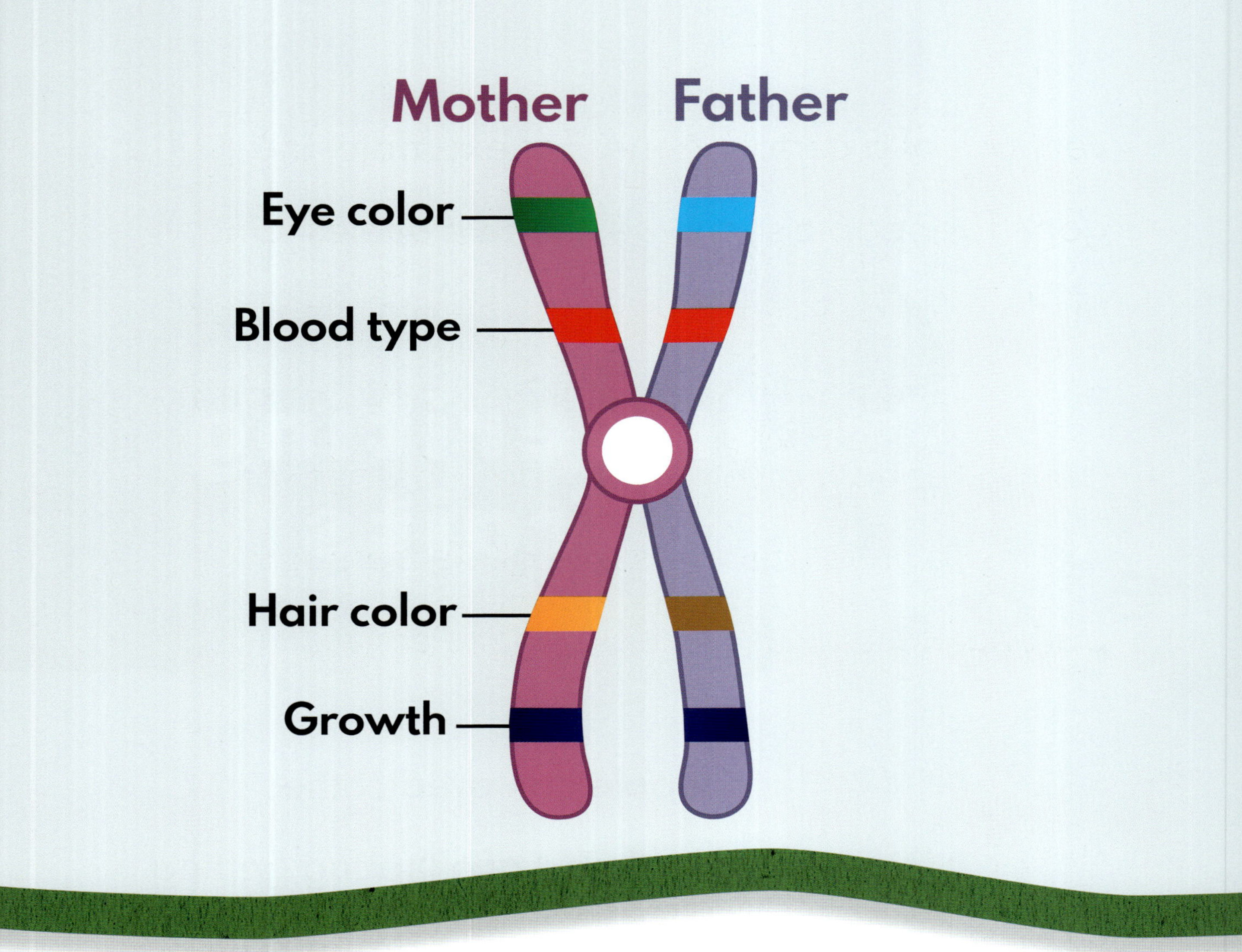

In a chromosome pair, one allele came from the mother and the other came from the father.

Each section of a Punnett square shows a different possible combination of the parents' genes. All squares together tell the likelihood of getting a trait. An allele is any of the possible versions of a certain gene. For example, the gene for people's hairline has two alleles. One allele is for a straight hairline. The other causes a V-shaped hairline, also called a widow's peak. No matter how many alleles are possible for a gene, a child only gets one allele from each parent. Most often, multiple genes control a trait.

Inside and Out

Not all alleles end up influencing someone's traits. Some alleles are considered dominant. Others are recessive. If there are two dominant alleles or one dominant and one recessive allele, the dominant trait will show. A recessive trait will show only if there are two recessive alleles.

A black Lab could have the alleles BB or Bb. A chocolate Lab will always have the alleles bb.

People often use capital and lowercase letters to represent alleles. Capital letters stand for dominant alleles. Lowercase letters stand for recessive alleles. In Labrador retrievers, black is the dominant fur color. It is represented by B. Chocolate is the recessive allele. It is represented by b. Puppies with BB or Bb alleles will have black fur. Only puppies with the alleles bb will be chocolate. Both parents must pass on the b allele.

Punnett Square

This Punnett square shows the alleles of two black Labradors. Both dogs carry a chocolate allele. Dominant black is B. Recessive chocolate is b. All of their offspring that inherit at least one B allele will be black. Each puppy has a 75 percent chance of being black. And each has a 25 percent chance that it will inherit two b alleles. If it does, it will be chocolate.

Some parents show a dominant trait. But they can pass on a recessive allele. These parents are called carriers. Labradors with Bb alleles are carriers of the chocolate color.

Why Does Genetics Matter?

Genetics is important for many reasons. It can help people watch out for health issues. Cancer, diabetes, and other diseases can be genetic.

Evolution

Over time, genes that help a species survive get passed on. Genes that don't help or aren't needed may stop being passed on. Over long periods of time, species change by passing on certain genes in a process called evolution.

Knowing if certain conditions run in a family can help people take steps to stay healthy and reduce the effects of certain genetic conditions.

Every person's genetic combination is unique!

People may be at higher risk if their parents or **ancestors** had a genetic condition. Someone at risk for cancer may do an extra test to check for it. Cancer can be easier to treat when noticed early. Someone at risk for diabetes may follow a careful diet. Eating healthy can help **prevent** diabetes.

Each person's genes are different. But everyone can benefit from learning about genetics. They can see what makes them unique!

Picture Biology

- The allele that causes a widow's peak is dominant.

- This Punnett square shows the likelihood of inheritance when one parent has two copies of the allele that causes a widow's peak and the other has no copies.

- All children will have a 100 percent chance of being Ww, which means that they will have a widow's peak.

- All children will also have a 100 percent chance of carrying the gene that does not cause a widow's peak. If they have children with someone else who has this gene, their offspring may not have a widow's peak.

Mother
w
W
W
w
Ww
Ww
Ww
Ww

Father

Glossary

ancestors
past generations of family members

genes
information in DNA passed from parents to offspring that affects how the offspring look and behave

genome
all of an individual's genes together

inherited
passed from parents to offspring

nucleus
the part of a cell that gives directions to the other parts

prevent
to avoid, stop, block, or slow down

Online Resources

To learn more about genetics, visit our free resource websites below.

Visit **abdocorelibrary.com** or scan this QR code for free Common Core resources for teachers and students, including vetted activities, multimedia, and booklinks, for deeper subject comprehension.

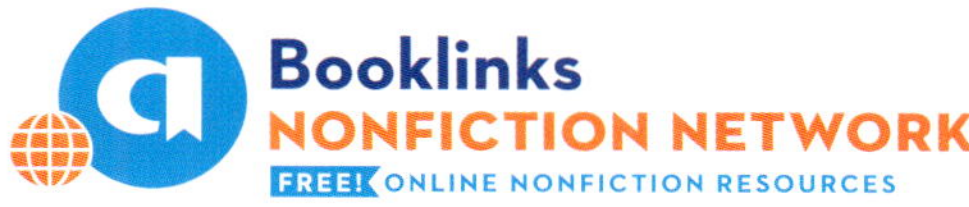

Visit **abdobooklinks.com** or scan this QR code for free additional online weblinks for further learning. These links are routinely monitored and updated to provide the most current information available.

Learn More

Cole, Joanna, and Bruce Degen. *The Magic School Bus Explores Human Evolution.* Scholastic, 2020.

The DNA Book. DK, 2020.

Index

alleles, 20–24

cells, 8, 14
chromosomes, 13–15, 20

DNA, 13, 14

genetics, 8, 11, 24, 27
genome, 9, 11

Labrador retrievers, 5–7,
  22–24

nucleus, 8, 14

parents, 5, 7–8, 19–26
Punnett square, 19–20, 23

Sulston, John, 11

traits, 16–17, 19–21, 24

About the Author

Emma Huddleston lives in the Twin Cities, Minnesota, with her husband. She enjoys reading, swing dancing, and writing books for young readers. She thinks genetics is fascinating and likes to see which traits are common in her family!